An independent critique
by

Aaron Ryan

Award-winning author of the bestselling alien invasion saga
Dissonance, the bestselling Christian dystopian saga *The
End,* the 9/11 historical fiction thriller *Forecast, The
Christian Kids Values, Identity & Affirmation* picture books,
and *God Is Not Santa*

Published in 2025, Edition 1.

eBook ISBN # eBook: 9781965372340 · Paperback ISBN #
9781965372357 · Hardcover ISBN # 9781965372364

Edited by CM LLC. Published independently.

Cover art by CM LLC.

This is a work of nonfiction. Any similarities to persons
living or dead, or actual events is purely coincidental.

For Sweeps, Bren & AJ:
my true loves.

Thank you for being the beautiful realization
of my deepest fantasies.

Examining The Lord of The Rings

Chapters

Note on A.I.

We live in an age of AI. Every day, more and more services spring up promising revolutionary and innovative results using artificial intelligence. The authoring industry is not immune to this.

I want every one of my readers to know that not once did I employ, nor will I *ever* employ, the use of AI to sculpt any part of any of my stories. Those who know me know that I am staunchly and adamantly opposed to such cheats.

I'm very proud to be a verified human. The ability to create is a gift that I was endowed by my Creator, and I will never forfeit that nor set it aside to propagate something synthetic and imitative.

Everything you've read by me in this saga, and in all my other works, is 100% entirely created by me, the genuine article. I'm a verified human, and always will be.

To my fellow authors, I urge you to preserve the sacred gift of human creation and never stoop to such lows. Always cherish this gift you've been given. If you encounter writer's block, take a break. Don't cop out. Don't take the road more traveled by. Don't cheat. Toe the line for all of us, and keep creation – *true* unadulterated creation – alive.

Long live humanity.

Sincerely,

Aaron Ryan,
Verified Human

Introduction

by Aaron Ryan

Introduction

With the releases of the Oscar-winning cinematic treasures from *New Line Cinemas*, the hype and interest in J.R.R. Tolkien's epic saga has been reinvigorated to such a degree that no movie series ever released will likely match its intensity.

My own interest in *The Lord of the Rings* spans decades. I remember reading *The Hobbit* first in junior high school and being intrigued by it. I remember reading its successor shortly thereafter and being absolutely spellbound. In fact, to be fair, "successor" is a terrible misnomer, and in fact a grievous underestimation of the most captivating fictional masterpiece of all time.

The Lord of the Rings reached deep down into my heart and catapulted my imagination into the furthest reaches of Middle-Earth. When I was first given the series in 1989 as a Christmas present, I was simply overjoyed to have my own copy (although I had already read it a few times from the library beginning in 1984). I could never imagine that an annual pilgrimage of plunging deep into the realm of Tolkien's genius would become my ritual.

Instinctively when winter would set in, I would reach once more for the enthralling trilogy on my bookshelf and immerse myself in it yet again. I remember burying my nose in the creases of the book and inhaling deeply the sweet fragrance of knowledge. There was a strangely pungent aroma permeating those books, and it wasn't just ink and paper. It was fantasy. It was imagination. It was *awe* to me.

I would go on to read that epic story every year without fail, and at this writing, I have read the entire trilogy over 100 times. Timeless passages have imprinted themselves in my memory and I often find myself recollecting and employing them in daily life and conversation. When I heard that Peter Jackson and *New Line Cinemas* were finally producing the entire opus in all its majesty and in, deservedly, three individual films, my heart leapt. "Well, it's about time," I thought. And simultaneously I was filled with all kinds of hopes and fears, anticipations and dreads, hoping that the visual deliverance of such a grand *oeuvre* would prove to meet all of my expectations. My brother will attest that prior to the midnight-screening on the day of the release of the first film, I was drooling. And he will also attest that throughout the length and breadth of the film, my jaw was a permanent fixture on the floor.

Even at points where I knew where the story would go, such as when Gandalf plunges down the "bottomless" pit under Khazad-dûm after the fiery Balrog (and to his seeming death below), I was seized with emotion. I knew full well Gandalf would not die, yet I honestly shed tears seeing that dramatic scene brought to life so powerfully. In each successive movie, I was brought to tears at some point, realizing the length and breadth the director went to realize Tolkien's visions onscreen. I will never forget the most powerful moment of the saga, when Samwise speaks words of summoned hope to Frodo, and then lifts and carries him up the slopes of Mount Doom. I get chills just thinking about it.

Tolkien's story, long ago, had wrought such immeasurable havoc on my preconceived notions of the standards of quality literature…I was unprepared at least, and blown away at best, for what rich treasures lay in the writing. From the onset of the story at Bilbo Baggins' party to Sam's return to Bag End after the departure at the Grey Havens, I was *enthralled*. It would be impossible for me to sum up how much this entire story means to me: I don't really know what it is.

Has each published book been soaked in a vat of magic? Have the stories been so laced with ingenuity

as to inflict the conscience with addictive fervor?
There is, indeed, *naught,* that can adequately explain
what this story means to myself and so many million
more readers worldwide. For the Tolkien fan, this is
sacred. It is drenched with meaning. It is *real*. It is a
tour de force, an awe-inspiring immersion, a
belonging to something genuinely nourishing.

Fiction and literature have truly seen more than their
fair share of fantasy. It is a genre of author-sing that
demands an incredibly expansive sense of
imagination and ingenuity. To create a world apart
from that which we know is an arduous task that
must be undertaken with strict guidelines, adherence
to new laws, and an understanding of the necessity
of gently introducing the reader into this new world.

You cannot simply whisk someone away to a
magical land and throw bizarre names and faces at
them and expect them to swallow it obediently. It
must be grounded in laws, in truth, and somewhat,
in reality. Madeline L'Engel, C.S. Lewis and Anne

McCaffrey knew this as well as J.R.R. Tolkien did, but Tolkien had a super-advantage of linguistics and history studies. The characters, the tongues, the names…all of them stemmed from a love of languages, in particular, and Tolkien ground this heritage into his creations with passion – whether the languages were old Norse, Tengwar, Daeron, Quenya or Sindarin – he made them all grounded in *reality*. One of the prime reasons why *The Lord of the Rings* is so incredibly sacred to me, (and, I'll wager, to others) is that it *feels* real. It makes complete sense. It's not a temporary spell cast over you – you close the last few pages of the book (when you do finally get there – the journey is of a pleasurably long duration!) and feel part of something wonderfully tangible that stays with you for the long haul.

There is, actually, nothing "fantasy" about *The Lord of the Rings*. I found myself believing that it actually existed, somewhere, sometime. I was not so much saturated by its imaginative scope as I was convinced of its literal presence in the pages of history. Gandalf could have been one of my great ancestors, for all I cared: all I wanted was to read it, shake my head in awe, and turn back to page one and start again. And I have done so for many years now. There is nothing else that has even touched the depth of his work, slaved over for several decades with true grit and passion. I will offend many when I say that *Harry Potter* is a cheap rip-off. In fact, all works of fantasy, if you really look close, tip their hat in one way or another to Tolkien's genius.

If this is your first time partaking of this epic tale, I invite you to separate, at the onset, what you have known about fact and fiction. Imagine for a moment that you could go back through a time portal to the same earthly plain that we live on today. I remain absolutely stalwart in my assertion that if you pinpoint your coordinates and time-plotting correctly, you will set yourself down in Bag End…or at the pinnacle of Orthanc…or by the dark, sad waters of Lake Nurnen in Mordor.

You will converse with hobbits, orcs, the Dark Lord, elves and wizards. Your heart will tremble at the *doom-doom* in the vast caverns of Moria, beat with adrenaline as you fly on the back of Gwaihir the Windlord, and leap with joy at the crowning of Aragorn.

No matter who you are, where you are, *what* you are…Middle-Earth will hook you - I guarantee it. It hooked me, and beginning in 2004, I began to devote a few years of my life to creating a keepsake edition of the *LOTR* for myself. Never to be sold; never to be promoted; simply to be enjoyed for all time, privately, by me.

I began by melding some of Tolkien's "lost" passages into his original work. Along with this, I painfully and cautiously integrated my own residential perspective of Middle-Earth in various other passages that I felt belonged. An avid and die-hard "re-" reader of *LOTR* would notice and hopefully appreciate them from the get-go. Let me also express from the onset that these added passages of my own were in no way intended as "corrective", replacement, or stemming from a notion that "he should have done it this way." On the contrary, Tolkien himself expressed in his forenote that there were some errors that were glossed over (which I then fixed, as per his desire, I'll wager). Some of these errors were pointed out by his son Christopher Tolkien in his excellent biographical works like *The Treason of Isengard* and *The War of the Ring*. Tolkien's son paid close attention to his father's notes, painstakingly researching the behind-the-scenes sculpture of *LOTR*.

If there are as many true "ringsgeeks" out there as I believe there to be, most of them would catch the changes rather fluidly. However, I am not omniscient or flawless by any stretch of the imagination; doubtless there inevitably remain some minor errors that hopefully do not confuse or distract. When I found the unedited text of all three books available online and began this journey, it was, by no means, precision at the outset. I undertook therefore to correct a plethora of typos and grammatical errors, but doubtless did not tackle every single one.

In terms of additions, they emanated only from a profound love of this work, in which I deeply desired to be a participant. I desired to take my own little time-travel and join Tolkien at creation. To be part of something so infinitely wondrous was probably never my right: however Tolkien dared me to be daring, and to stretch my imagination.

I decided to take him up on that challenge.

It was quite practical, really. For example, there is an invaluable piece of history in the chapter "The Quest of Erebor" (from Tolkien's book, *Unfinished*

Tales) that involves Gandalf's summary of events preceding the adventure of Bilbo Baggins that patently factored into the steps leading up to the War of the Ring.

I simply incorporated this as a "hindsight is 20-20" perspective in *The Return of the King*, Book Six, Chapter VI, "The Designs of Wizardry." I found this piece of the grand puzzle to be indispensable in my assembly. I subsequently could not then subtract Samwise's storytelling account as recaptured by Christopher Tolkien, from the last chapter of the trilogy, "The Grey Havens." It is such a beautiful segment of a continuing story; I restored it after Sam's return home.

There are also punctuations of comedy that Tolkien inserted and then withdrew. Christopher Tolkien detailed them, and I inserted them. By no means is *The Lord of the Rings* a lighthearted tale of comedy – it is dark and mysterious, lighthearted and obvious at the same time. It is this melancholy mix that makes the story so well-rounded. However, re-importing these rare points of humor, such as Gandalf's quip back to Legolas on the slopes of Caradhras, were, I felt, complimentary to Tolkien's vision, and enjoyable enough to include in my own private edition.

Aside from that, I created narratives which serve as a follow-up to some Tolkien references made at earlier points, which he never revisited.

I simply hammered out scenes, much I felt as Tolkien would have: scenes that compliment and do not distract. Scenes that provide a more rounded picture of the saga and that bring to conclusion prior said references.

Faramir's talk with Frodo after the war of the ring ("laughing at old grief") and Gandalf's and Aragorn's meeting with Faramir (explaining Denethor's fall to inform Faramir what happened while he was in the

Houses of Healing) are prime examples of these.

Additionally, Gandalf's conversation with Frodo about Gwaihir after the Council of Elrond served to eliminate a recurring question I've heard time and time again in forums and *LOTR* groups online as to simplifying the mission to eradicate the ring. I wanted to help eliminate the path of least resistance and further explain why the journey of secrecy was so necessary. Gwaihir and the eagles could not simply "perform a fly-by."

All in all, I yearned to be part of Tolkien's vision of creation. That, in short, is what he does: he spawns creativity. And while my short interjections will fall dreadfully short of Tolkien's brilliance, they were intended more as a form of partnership in something wonderful. That was my sole aim in this endeavor.

Doubtless, the purists who consider themselves as inexorably allegiant, if they ever read my keepsake, would not be able to divorce themselves from the original work, as they were most likely unable to do with some of Peter Jackson's deviations in movie form, or *The Ring of Power* Amazon Prime Video productions. I am not asking them to do so, and they should feel free to dispute my contributions. For that I commend them.

However I can assure everyone that I created my own private version because of a mutual appreciation for the sacredness of the original text, and I treated my project reverently and carefully.

All in all, my compositions represented but a minute fraction of the mammoth of beautiful narrative, and did not appear, to me, to be intrusive (speaking as objectively as possible). And now? I get to enjoy it year after year, which I have done every holiday season since I was a boy, with my new 'Expanded Edition,' my personal keepsake.

As an author myself, inspired by Tolkien, I have at diverse times attempted to structure out a continuing story that carries forward the ending of this trilogy. However, I have painfully discovered that such a project is simply beyond me.

My literary and creative prowess, as complimented as they may have been, are simply overmatched by J.R.R. Tolkien. I have therefore attempted to unite my creativity with his through my very heartfelt *private* project, which was truly a labour of love. It resulted in a red-leather-bound and foil-stamped keepsake that is glorious to look upon and to enjoy.

Not to imply any sort of spiritual "habitation," but in a way, since his passing in 1973, I have always thought, "what if just a little bit of his spirit passed into me?" (1973 was my birth year). I have always felt a kinship with the dreams, vision and fantasy he bequeathed to us through *The Lord of the Rings.* As I could not seem to create a continuation, I resorted to merging some of my own ideas into his story, with the intention of being a loyal part of his dream, not interrupting it.

My edition came 50 years precisely since his passing, I dedicated it privately to John Ronald Reuel Tolkien.

If I could demand that everyone on earth read two things, I would demand that first, they read the Bible. There is richness, hope, joy, grace and truth, above all else, there. There is *absolute,* indefatigable, and unarguable reality there: the history of God's interaction with mankind, the beautiful gospels of Jesus Christ Almighty, our Lord and Savior, and the accounts of lives transformed by His grace, are essential to growing, learning, maturing, and attaining to the whole measure of righteousness. Supplemental to all of this, there exist a plethora of rich works written by inspired authors the world over. One of those was J.R.R. Tolkien.

I would secondly demand that all would read

Tolkien's trilogy and come to know the joys of beautiful literature, hope, victory and maturation through trials. It is a heavy tale of defeat and victory, joy and sadness, love and loss, death and rebirth…and although Tolkien himself states that he disliked allegory, you will no doubt find plentiful references to biblical truths therein.

It is, next to the Bible, the most beautiful thing I have ever read…and then re-read a hundred times again. It is my prayer that this beautiful story would captivate and inspire you as it has done me.

Those who have enjoyed the recent series from *New Line Cinemas* as much as I have, were they to pick up my keepsake, would also enjoy the pictures captured from various scenes interspersed from the movies (captured and included from public domain), now embedded in each of the three books where pertinent to the running narrative.

All in all, may *The Lord of the Rings*, the quintessential work of fantasy fiction and such a timeless classic, continue to amaze and inspire you to no end. Hopefully, reading through my little book here, Tolkien's vision will not be impeded or impaired by mine.

For my part I strove to articulate just how much this marvelous author and wondrous story mean to me. It is certainly not the Bible, the most sacred and real work of all, but it is nonetheless deeply sacred and real to many.

May you, the reader, feel it as deeply as I have, for many years to come.

Sincerely,

An Examination of the Lord of the Rings

An independent critique by Aaron Ryan

Examining The Lord of the Rings

THESIS

"By root and twig, but it is a strange business: up sprout a little folk that are not in the old lists, and behold! The Nine forgotten riders reappear to hunt them, and Gandalf takes them on a great journey, and Galadriel harbours them in Caras Galadon, and Orcs pursue them down all the leagues of Wilderland: indeed they seem to be caught up in a great storm. I hope they weather it!"

Such words by a major player in the epic saga, *The Lord of the Rings* may do its tale and theme minimal justice to be sure, but the monumental masterpiece by J.R.R. Tolkien can hardly be price-tagged. The major player in the aforementioned quote is "Treebeard," speaking in the vast buttresses of Fangorn Forest to his three-foot-tall guests, Meriadoc ("Merry") Brandybuck and Peregrin ("Pippin") Took, of the Shire. Described later on (in the third part of a trilogy of books that comprise the series) and addresses as "Eldest," his perspective, spanning eons and generations, dare not be second-guessed.

THE AUTHOR

Yet behind such an ageless character lies the master sculptor, Mr. Tolkien himself. For 14 long years, from approximately 1936 to 1949, and even then until 1954 when it was published, Tolkien wove the greatest, most uncontested fictional tale of all time. Matchless in its scope, literary genius, fantastical depth and imaginative reach, *The Lord of the Rings* has stood the test of time as the pinnacle and cornerstone of its genre, and has become the model from which all prospective successors spring. Frankly, when compared to other notable authors of his time and after, the appropriate word to use to describe his victory is "eclipsing:" others pale exceptionally by comparison. Authors from Piers

Anthony to C.S. Lewis to J.K. Rowling of the current "Harry Potter" series, and even to George Lucas of "Star Wars" fame, will reluctantly admit that their spin-offs contain some derivatives of that which epitomized Tolkien's grandeur. In fact, let me so bold as to say that every successive effort at fantasy-fiction has been marginally successful at best; grossly pitiful rehash at worst. Successors come across as cheap rip-off's. And even moderate successes contain suspicious similarities or imitations both in character formation and storyline structure. Whereas Tolkien is natural and earthy, his imitators scream mechanical aridity. Something is lacking in their works that Tolkien makes up for, by far. In short, J.R.R Tolkien and *The Lord of the Rings* remain the undisputed kings of the fantasy hill.

THE LANGUAGE OF THE STORY

In stark contrast to the overwhelming majority of his successors, either because of the sheer enormity of time devoted to his baby, or because of simply lackluster replications along similar storylines, *The*

Lord of the Rings stands perpetually poised on the edge, on the fence dividing the real from the imitation. Whereas in other works, the reader is unquestionably in an alien/fantasy world, the *Rings* reader is left happily reeling from the sheer vastness of the tale, and forced to probe deeper into the actual possibility of the existence of Middle-earth. For the geographical and historical foundations of Tolkien's epic lay rooted in tangibles (the story is not too distantly removed from similar known medieval and Gothic elements), and yet also in intangibles (the story is stand-alone enough to create an air of credible mystery). Cloaked in comprehensive, imaginative genius and yet practical in its implications, *The Lord of the Rings* instantly grabs the reader's attention and does not surrender it until its powerful conclusion in Book Three of the series. This is a direct result of its mysterious location in time and space: the reader is forced to investigate.

To make any good tale great, and so increase its rank, a compelling storyline is needed. But most artists end up striving to develop a microwave recipe for intrigue, and thus blindside themselves by ignoring the story's most crucial element: depth. Their stories subsequently then become an overly giddy skip through a bleak, uninteresting campaign. Not so with "The Lord of the Rings." Carefully chiseling his epic over 14 slow, agonizing, formative years, Tolkien placed it on his anvil and then painstakingly hammered out a riveting, successful tale, and compounded its impact by reinforcing depth every step of the way. In one sense, the reader is prompted to accept "given" realities, such as the ongoing strife between the Elves and the Dwarves, or the multi-millennial prologue which is assumed as a buildup for the tale, laid down in his successive work, "The Silmarillion." However, since the reader has not yet been introduced to the pre-history explained by this later book (it was not published itself until 1977), Tolkien masterfully generates a stalwart trust by familiarizing his readers with the characters' geography, culture, personalities, functions, and overall purpose of presence. And he does it with a methodical grace, too: sophisticated and thorough, yet elementary enough for a reader of any age to appreciate it without feeling condescended to. He doesn't throw silly talking dragons, cackling witches and flying unicorns (purple, of course) at the reader and insist that they arbitrarily accept them, and neither is he nonchalant: he is precise in his presentation of an authentic, tasteful and inhabited world. The foundation is laid through rational groundbreaking and introduction, appealing descriptions and a sincere appraisal of all of his creations: not to be toyed with, and certainly not toys. They are all living, breathing beings who are joyful and sad, content and melancholy, routine and proud. It is this manipulation of standard cookie-cutter fantasy that sets Tolkien's characters in a league of their own and gives them great depth.

Their names are then icing on the cake. And yet those are not merely gumball candy randomly dispersed: they are methodically, symbolically and linguistically applied based on a profound grasp of Old English mastered by Tolkien while a professor at Oxford University. Appealing to the reader's (and his own) sense of intriguing phonetics, all of the gracious inventions and personalities of his saga – in all three books, whether cameo or consistent characters – have very purposeful names. Along the same lines, geographical regions and other landmarks like hills, valleys, mountains, rivers, forests, lakes, caves, passages, etc., have consistent linguistic attention: all are crafted purposefully and with a heavy dose of delicate beauty. This, additionally, leaves the reader wishing for a Middle-earth that is just around the corner, accessible…real, and full of depth. And as if that wasn't enough, Tolkien supplies painstakingly-detailed maps, done severally over with the utmost attention and the finest pen strokes. Had they been done any more finely, no doubt they would resemble high-altitude satellite photographs of an as-yet unknown landscape, an undiscovered country. The subsequent effect is residual: Middle-earth does in fact exist somewhere, some time, and thus the reader is compelled to revisit and re-explore.

Equally textually stimulating are the beautiful and plentiful renderings of landscapes. From the most minute detail of vegetation in the undergrowth, to the generous helpings of towering mountains, rolling fields, and swift-moving currents of great rivers, the appetite for an extended trek augments considerably. The reader is enticed and lured into a limitless range of absolute and profound beauty in this terrain of grandeur.

In a literary sense, Tolkien "sings" to his "listeners" through expansive imagery. His extensive vocabulary and artistic rendering of language make for exquisite reading. Perhaps one of the greatest passages as a lasting tribute to Tolkien's linguistic genius, I present this excerpt from the third book of the trilogy, *The Return of the King*:

> *"...as the sweet influence of the herb stole about the chamber, it seemed to those who stood by that a keen wind blew through the window, and it bore no scent, but was an air wholly fresh and clean and young, as if it had not before been breathed by any living thing and came new-made from snowy mountains*

> *high beneath a dome of stars, or from*
> *shores of silver far away washed by seas*
> *of foam."*

Truly powerful imagery. Were it possible to verifiably transplant a living being inside the pages of a book to the vast poetic splendour behind the black and white pages, then this author would be the exclusive recipient of an award for such a feat.

THE CHARACTERS AND THE CULTURES

Over 1,000 pages in length, *The Lord of the Rings* is the landmark and cornerstone of inventive bravado for fantasy-fiction. Gripping in its tale of good versus evil, unbelievably stimulating in its voyage from innocence to experience, and unquestionably exhilarating in its descriptive breadth, again, it is the uncontested victor of its arena. Readers identify with the timid protagonist in Frodo Baggins; they cheer on the wizened, bent champion in Gandalf, and they help swing Andúril, the legendary sword of Aragorn. They feel themselves in the circumstances of duress such as before the mammoth Balrog on the bridge of Khazad-dûm; or in the cold peril of the Paths of the Dead; or inside Orodruin on the threshold of the Cracks of Doom. And once they've survived, they breathe a collective sigh of relief with the victorious member of the Fellowship, and thus claim a victory for themselves as well. There is grief and empathy for Eowyn, the "cold maiden of the Rohirrim"; curiosity and fear of Shelob, "last child of Ungoliant to trouble the unhappy world"; and intrigue and fascination with Ghan-buri-Ghan and the Pukel-men of Druadan Forest. From the moment the reader first makes acquaintance with a particular character, Tolkien immerses them in its ways, behavior, culture, history, nuances, etc., and the reader in turn pledges undying allegiance to that character, whether good or bad – it has become an integral role in the life of the story from that point on. The reader in turn becomes voluntary governor of this imaginary world they now own. They lock in on that character's essential function and role, and their allegiance does not fail them: Tolkien delivers. The diversity and widespread community populating

Middle-earth create a unique harmony that challenges the reader to open his mind to strange new races and fascinating lifestyles.

Exceedingly diverse in its overlay, Middle-earth represents, among other things, four main kindreds: Elves, Men, Dwarves, and Hobbits. In the introductory premise, the "theme poem" of the saga, the first three of these are mentioned. However, being that the protagonist throughout is the diminutive Frodo Baggins, and that we are quickly immersed in their culture, hobbits become the forerunners of the story. Elrond said it best in the chapter, "The Council of Elrond" (in the first book, *The Fellowship of the Ring*) when he said, "Now is the hour of the Shire-folk: when they arise from their quiet fields to shake the towers and the counsels of the great. Who of all the wise could have foreseen it?" In the introductory chapters of *The Hobbit,* (Tolkien's prelude to the *Rings* series), the author gracefully introduces a quaint, furry-footed little folk that are secure in their environment and have no wish for adventures, thank you. They

can come across as both patently rude and obscenely

polite in the same instance: and it is this assembly of

peculiar oddities that fascinates the reader with this

eccentric folk. The hobbits are a tight-knit

community of farmers, gardeners and millwrights

that patronizes only itself and relegates itself to

secrecy and isolation in a lush countryside known as

"The Shire." And that is how they prefer it: eating

bountiful (and plentiful) meals a day, capable of

downing consecutive mugs of ale without the

slightest hint of intoxication, and wreathing

themselves in pipe-smoke ("Longbottom Leaf," to

be precise) at all hours of the day. The Shire is the

perfect haven for these bustling yet carefree

denizens. Readers enjoy the quaint Londonesque

brisqué of snotty yet patient condescension of the

hobbits to themselves and others. Their ambience

is contagious, and every reader, honest to himself,

secretly wishes they could hop on over the

Brandywine River, saunter up the road past The

Green Dragon Inn, and on up to Hobbiton. They

long to kick up their feet for a cozy, pleasant

vacation in front of the fire under hill. All in all, this quiet little folk, fenced off from the dangers of the world, is ready and primed for a rude awakening: just the recipe Gandalf the Wizard specializes in and has in store for young Frodo Baggins, who becomes the Hobbit poster-child.

Although not a specific race, Wizards are an integral component in "Rings." Wizards are the movers and shakers of the chess-pieces in the saga, and while three are specifically (and heavily) involved, there are purported to be five of the order in total. Known as "The Istari", they "appeared first after the Great Ships came over the Sea [to Middle-earth]." Again, spoken by the Ent Treebeard to Merry and Pippin, his account is authoritative. Sent by the Valar of Numenor to be the guardians of peace and freedom in Middle-earth, they were endowed with special gifts and abilities, along with expansive knowledge and unnatural wisdom. The main two wizards predominantly responsible for the upkeep of the world are Saruman the White (also known as

"Curunir"), and Gandalf the Grey, or "Mithrandir." Gandalf assigns himself the role of a sort of wandering, nomad custodian who responsibly oversees specific branches and breeds of life. Saruman, however, establishes himself at the fortress of Isengard (or "Angrenost") at the butt-end of the Misty Mountains. He is proclaimed and elected to be the Chief of the "Wise," a council including himself, Gandalf, and several of the leading Elven-lords of various regions. The third mention is of a sort of vagabond wizard known as Radagast the Brown. His only appearance is that of a cameo, but in that brevity the reader learns that this wizard possesses extraordinary gifts with birds and beasts. Though Radagast's appearance is brief and forgettable, his presence in the story lends a subtle weight to the history and operation of Middle-earth. There is something there that we are not told, and that in and of itself augments the sense of a "pre-history" and established weight of Middle-earth.

Tolkien does not flaunt the wizards' gifts, however; he tends rather to embrace their humanity and simplicity, particularly as in the case of Gandalf, ergo making them much more practical and embraceable. Rather than having the wizards chant silly, incomprehensible spells with the customary waving of the wand, he allows the reader's imagination to expound and embellish those deeds within the spectrum of their own imagination, thus encouraging personal ownership of each respective character. This is another of Tolkien's glaring trademarks: he does not give the story or character away at any point – he leaves to the imagination of the reader anything society and/or other works of fiction tend to "standard-issue."

Saruman, like Boromir of Minas Tirith, eventually falls prey to the allure of the Ring, and in doing so forfeits his place among the Wise. His desire, one for rule, places him at odds with the other free peoples and painfully assures them of his treachery. Again, we see the dreadful working power of the

Ring's evil, and its effect even on those accounted "wise." Gandalf himself, discerningly so, refuses to accept custodianship of the Ring, even as a freely-offered gift (as does Galadriel, the Elven-queen), and so endears himself all the more to the reader – they are secure in the knowledge that he is benevolent and wise, and moreover, "on their side." There is no fear of betrayal. Altogether, the Wizards represent another intriguing branch of both Middle-earth's intelligentsia and its populace, which must be reckoned with throughout the great quest. As Bilbo Baggins was noted to say, "Do not meddle in the affairs of wizards; for they are subtle, and quick to anger…" Very descriptive of the power and sway attributed and entrusted to these of Tolkien's creation.

The Elves themselves have been around for a very long time. There are different branches, such as the Noldor and the Silvan Elves, yet kindreds differ little. They cannot die of natural causes, but they can be wounded and killed in battle. Their eyes have seen age after age of war and peace, they are deeply reclusive and highly distrustful of other races, i.e., Dwarves, and they were the first pioneers and inhabitants of Middle-earth. In the context of *The Lord of the Rings*, there are a relative few, a handful at best, of Elven-lord representatives who recall the former might and glory of the "Elder Days". Elrond of Rivendell and Galadriel and Celeborn of Lothlorien are the chief few of these. Their purposes for lingering in Middle-earth are shrouded in melancholy; perhaps sadly reflecting on past history and bygones of Middle-earth, "suffering the long defeat" (as Galadriel so eloquently puts it at one point), they await the day when they will irrevocably depart from Middle-earth for the distant shores of Numenor, over the Sea. For when Sauron of old fashioned the One Ring to rule the nineteen others, their works of grandeur, wrought with the three rings they were given, were laid bare. They could therefore avail themselves of these no longer, and their ring-produced artistry would thus no longer flower, being now revealed, and so corruptible, to Sauron. Ergo their bitter decision to leave.

Elves are a proud race. In some senses, to be an Elf is a euphemism for royalty. Theirs is the heritage of the first-born. They are the immortals. Because of this, the reader is allowed very few scant glimpses into a deeply proud lineage filled with many notable characters, but more insight can be gained from the various appendices supplementing the saga at the end of the third book of the series, *The Return of the King,* or in Tolkien's work of pre-history, *The Silmarillion.*

Dwarves, as the second-born, have a lengthy and proud history as well. Sundered from civilization, they share many similar notes of contained arrogance, though their descent through the ages is marked more by isolation and fierce racial preservation. They are turbulently protective of their species, particularly their females, keeping them so well-hidden that they are often mistaken for males. The Dwarves isolate themselves to caverns and mines and storehouses of riches and gold; for covetousness is their defining characteristic (at least by perception), and their coat of arms. Perched like hens on their nest-eggs, they protect their hoards with materialistic obsession. It is this mania that drives the Dwarves into the dark caverns of the Mines of Moria, and to Mount Erebor, in search of greater plunder, and of course, mithril, the most precious metal in the world. Dark fate awaits them in both locations, but they are so blinded by greed it escapes them until the end. Consequently, the fierce pursuit of worldly good breeds division between themselves and the Elves, since the Dwarves, by perception, mar more than they make, being constantly on the hunt for deeper caverns, richer vaults and hidden, untapped chasms of treasure. During their fateful mining expedition to Moria under the Misty Mountains, the Dwarves do not help this perception and division by stirring up a ferocious demon of the underworld, the vicious Balrog of Morgoth, Flame of Udun.

Being a matter of pre-history as well, little is recorded of the giving of the Seven Rings of Power to the Dwarves. However, these Rings, being succoured to the power of the Dark Lord of Mordor, also become ultimately more a matter of legend than of life.

If the *middle* in "Middle-earth" suggests chronology, then it stands to reason that the present age is passing. The Elves so note this, and realize with melancholy that the race of men is quickly coming into its own as the dominant species and the beneficiaries of the future realm of Middle-earth, as well as the modern realm. Steeped in tradition, their various people share a common allegiance of humanity. The reader readily identifies with the struggles, victories and behaviors as most closely resembling their own. The people of Gondor are inherently related to the Eorlingas of Rohan, and Rohan's inhabitants are intrinsically linked to the people of the North. Cumulatively they all represent the coming rule of simple humanity, bereft of Elves and ignorant of other "lower" forms of life. But the circle is complete with mankind's ascension to the prominence.

One of the main cruxes of *The Lord of the Rings* is the inevitable ascent to the throne of Gondor by Aragorn, son of Arathorn, descendant of Earnur, the last reigning king of Gondor before the Stewards officially inherited government. Readers will embrace the sovereign right granted the man, and Aragorn's nobility endears them to the trail that he blazes towards his own coronation. His valiance and unswerving devotion to all that is good in Middle-earth is closely matched by comparable personifications of nobility from other peoples: notably, Eomer of Rohan, Prince Imrahil of Dol Amroth, and Faramir, son of Denethor, Steward of Gondor. The race of humanity, the race of man, is quickly becoming the backbone and the centerpiece of Middle-earth, and the dominant species, as all others merge slowly into obsolescence.

Early on in their history, however, Sauron was highly successful in seducing nine kings and rulers into accepting his gifts of nine rings of power. These men were slowly mutated and twisted, aligned unto his wickedness by their desire for power. They ultimately passed into the world of shadow, becoming the Black Riders, the Ringwraiths, the Nazgûl. The race of men therefore has been tainted by lust for power, and susceptible to corruption. This has a dramatic effect in augmenting Aragorn's nobility and underscoring his rightful place of humanity's redeemer: readers will understand this.

Punctuating the terrain are diverse creatures and peoples who come and go and who represent the salt-and-pepper of the *Rings* feast: their presence adds further spice and diversity. Their alignment with good or evil is quickly established; there are seldom any neutral characters. Good, like the Pukel-men of Druadan Forest, the great eagle Gwaihir the Windlord, the great Ents of Fangorn Forest, and the horses of Rohan, i.e., Gandalf's horse Shadowfax. And albeit eerie and questionable at first, the King of the Dead beyond Dwimorberg establishes himself as an ally, allegiant to Aragorn, heir of Isildur. Or evil, like the Watcher in the Water outside Moria, the Nine Ringwraiths and their Witch-King, the Orcs, the Balrog of Morgoth, the bird-spies of Saruman, and the favorite mystery character introduced in *The Hobbit:* the twisted creature Gollum.

Together, each species, whether making a cameo or recurring appearance, presents a wide palette of tasteful representation; the presentation of extensive biology assigned to Middle-earth. They entreat the reader to timely characters which Tolkien introduces at precise, methodical junctures. Each is complimentary in their own unique way to the indelible structure that is Middle-earth.

THE POETRY

Poetry remains yet another potent weapon in Tolkien's arsenal of literary brilliance. He presents several oratory juggernauts that are fraught with a trove of richness, such as his well-known opus on Earendil the Mariner (presented in the chapter *Many Meetings* in the first book of the series): hardly a trifle, it has received substantial acclaim even independent of the trilogy. Poetry is a recurring gem that dots the horizon of the main narrative and graces the reader with flawless imagery and impressive, alternative storytelling. These works are seldom idyllic; they are by and large historic in expression, recounting the history of Middle-earth in most forms. The poetry is never a mere byproduct either: it is almost as though the story has been structured around these intermittent gems. Their brevity belies their potency however: fleeting and printed in italics, the reader might be tempted to evade them and regard them as unnecessary intrusions. But in doing so, one misses an incalculable treasury of linguistic expression, of grammatical perfection, of prose in action, of great creative gold. Even from the silly, child-friendly poetic caperings of Tom Bombadil, the reader can extract extensive culture and personality that the regular narrative might have otherwise given away. Be that as it may, I do not wish to detract from the fluidity and articulative power of the body text either: readers are constantly entreated to extraordinary dialogues, lengthy depictions of scenery, and what not. But in and of itself, the poetry accounts for a substantial portion of the tale's immeasurable splendour: every one is a pristine prism of the same incomparable diamond.

Tolkien, in several of his poems, does not adhere to the cut-and-dry cookie-cutter poetic structure either. He often uses offset rhyming and a fluctuating flow that is extremely unique: none of them are run-of-the-mill in any way. In some senses he breaks the mold on poetry as we have been brought up to identify it. Stretching the confines of our limited tastes, he blows wide open the naïve notion that poetry needs to conform to a certain pattern. Many of his works represent Tolkien's own groundbreaking approach to creation, that of something never perceived, never fathomed. These characteristics and approaches further elevate Tolkien above and beyond all other authors.

THE RING

Throughout the three books, the reader is presented with multiple roadblocks and challenges. The quest Frodo Baggins and Company embark upon is fraught with peril and beset with foes. Yet quickly underlying symbolisms and messages spring up which inform the reader that despite the enormity of forces arrayed against the Fellowship, the Company's real true enemy is amongst them. Fourteen long years of penning a gargantuan tale of a far-away world filled with innumerable creatures and races, good and bad, and the driving force behind all the madness is the miniscule circle of gold known as The One Ring. The irony is blatant. Tolkien subtly and repeatedly encourages his readers, vicariously through the story's "Wise", not to fall prey to the allure of the Ring. And should the reader possess a stubborn, lustful vein, there are the graphic reminders of the human warrior Boromir, the former hobbit Gollum, and the once wise and respected member of the elite, Saruman the Wizard. Because of their own weaknesses and obsession with The One Ring, a tragic plight became their fate.

That the nemesis among them is so potent and yet so infinitesimal is not lost among the confederates. Indeed Boromir, before succumbing to its dreadful enticement, once says that it is "strange that we should suffer so much fear and doubt over such a little thing." The Ring's Maker, the Dark Lord Sauron, while seemingly remote and nonetheless an ominous threat garrisoned in his bastion of darkness at Barad-dur, himself poses only an inkling of the threat he would wield were the Ruling Ring to return to his hand. And should another valiant soul lay claim to victory and attempt to overthrow Sauron by the power of the One Ring, Sauron would fall and yet a new "Sauron" would emerge in the victor. A gross dichotomy is therefore evident to the reader. The Ring is a force of great power to defeat Sauron, yet to wield it, one would have to become the Dark Lord. The same manifestations of evil are then given new flesh as a garment and the same threat still festers. The solution then is evident: this tiny Ring, so seemingly harmless and yet so apparently deadly, must be destroyed. Elrond himself wisely says at one point, "I fear to take the Ring to hide it. I will not take the Ring to wield it." This paradox of a mighty heirloom so potently dangerous creates a highly suspenseful storyline, one the reader can appreciate.

Tolkien therefore skillfully weaves an intrepid thread of cat-and-mouse chases through the vast and lush leagues of Middle-earth, to the only possible destination for deliverance: Mount Doom, where the fires are hot enough to destroy the Ring and thus eliminate this cyclical threat once and for all. Therefore is born the Fellowship of the Nine Walkers, who, including Frodo, contain the faithful servant Samwise Gamgee, Merry and Pippin, also of the Shire, Gandalf the Grey, Aragorn the Ranger, Boromir of Gondor, Legolas the Elf and Gimli the Dwarf. Their multiple storylines interweave through the second book of the series, *The Two Towers*, and the third, *The Return of the King*, until they reunite, having been scattered and separated at the conclusion of the first book, *The Fellowship of the Ring*. This lengthy journey is the perfect stage-setter for the introduction of the various peoples and cultures that populate the landscapes, and it breeds a highly-plausible storyline that the reader can wholeheartedly embrace. This journey necessitates Tolkien's introductions of said people into the narrative, allowing the reader to learn and grasp the whole of Middle-earth.

Appealing to our senses of right and wrong, of addiction and resistance, of fantasy and reality, we know that we cannot use the Ring, however tempting that notion might be. Along with the protagonists, we are resigned to fight the long battle and destroy the Ring in the fires of Mount Doom.

RELIGIOUS UNDERTONES

My own Christianity and faith in Jesus Christ leads me to broach this new subject and major element which runs in an undercurrent throughout the saga, as it is arguably an essential one. I am in no way implying that that was Tolkien's intent; however the signals of parallels are unmistakably present, and, truthfully, delightful. Whether implied or imagined, it is noticeable on many occasions, and standard Judeo-Christian practitioners will, as I have, draw immediate and fascinating analogies (although Tolkien detested them) between the story's undertones and the messages from the Holy Bible.

For one example, note the main theme of good versus evil. While a major underlying thematic crux of any well-written story involving conflict, it rings especially true in Tolkien's saga. The forces arrayed on both sides of the spiritual fence are vast. But consider the names of the main two key representatives of good and evil: good, being Gandalf, and evil, being Sauron. God's name coincidentally begins with a "G", and Satan's with an "S." Gandalf's begins with a "G", and Sauron's with an "S." Consider the dwelling place of Sauron: The Dark Tower. Consider the translation of Tolkien's created name of a barren plain in Sauron's realm of Mordor: "Udun". Once translated, that's "hell." Readers who can identify, as I can, with the life, death and resurrection of Jesus Christ (God taking the form of man, dying on the cross and then resurrecting) will no doubt find a dynamic parallel in Gandalf "dying" in the mines of Moria and then coming back to life again, more powerful than before. The use of the old King James-era dialect in several passages, notably in the latter two books: words such as "hath", "ye", "whithersoever," and "nay" will immediately recall the King James Translation of the Bible. Furthermore, a few passages in and of themselves sound near-identical to Biblical passages. For instance, in the Chapter "The Shadow of the Past" (during which Gandalf recounts the majority of pertinent history preceding the current dilemma with the Ring), Gandalf explains to Frodo that "whereas the light perceives the very heart of the darkness, its own secret has not been discovered," which bears a striking resemblance to John 1:5 from the Holy Bible: "And the light shineth in the darkness, but the darkness comprehendeth it not." This is almost a veritable mirror in this instance. Additionally, there is the far-off, timeless shore of Numenor (called also "The Undying Lands"), which seems to be Tolkien's euphemism for heaven, and the allusion is not entirely ambiguous. However it is also a sufficient correlation that Gandalf dies and goes there…and that the Elves, a dying race, leave for Numenor.

A dynamically compelling example which can be interpreted as a religious undertone is the issue of Gollum's obsession with the Ring of Power. The Biblical equivalent is addiction to sin, and any warm-blooded Christian who has had even a minor struggle with a thorn in their flesh can relate to the frightening metamorphosis Smeagol-Gollum undergoes in his lust-filled slavery to the corruption of the Ring.

Reasoning behind all of those congruencies might be derived from a closer probe into the Author's past. His religious orientation is known to be one of devout Catholicism and he had close associates and fraternal "spiritual" confidants the likes of C.S. Lewis (the notable Christian author of *The Chronicles of Narnia* series). Both Lewis and Tolkien, among others, belonged to a members-only think-tank of scholarly gentleman known affectionately as "The Inklings", where they would peruse each other's works, chit-chat on literary insight with passionate abandon, and spurn each other on to greater mastery of artistic expression. Lewis himself went on to substantial fame with his *Narnia* series.

Altogether the saga couples the physical with the spiritual (or at least the ethereal), and the two become inseparable. Corruption to the Ring, and usage thereof, makes a living being "fade" in time, as is the case with the Ringwraiths.

And exposure to the negative forces of the ethereal, namely the Ringwraiths, as is the case with Frodo on Weathertop, makes one fade as well, passing them into the realm of the undead: without a doubt a state of torment, and of indefinite, abysmal slavery to the Ring and the Dark Lord.

Ultimately, some questions about the supposed religiosity of the undercurrent will remain unanswered. But sufficient allusions along a spiritual plain do keep the reader probing deeper into the theological undercurrent of the series.

SUMMARY

For 15 long years of his life, John Ronald Reuel Tolkien, on a typewriter in his garage study, wrought a magnificent tale of epic proportions. In settings pastoral and alternatively, pseudo-medieval, the protagonists venture out on a quest that the Author shrewdly beat out over a slow flame. Diligent and persistent in his aim, J.R.R. Tolkien gave birth to an unapproachable, invincible saga that would thrill and delight for years to come. In truth, to undertake a project of such mammoth proportions is not just courageous, it is exceedingly ambitious and risky. Countless other projects through the years doubtless fell by the wayside, abandoned by their dreamers as unattainable and risky. Tolkien risked…and attained.

The Lord of the Rings stands perpetually perched upon the highest eyrie, the apex and zenith of creative genius, like an eagle with its talons sunk deep into the prey of competition.   J.R.R. Tolkien's timeless classic, slow-cooked with care, just the right recipe for those displeased and broken from the harsh realities of the present and searching for meaningful escapism, delivers. It is not simply a time-killing excursion to temporarily steal affections and attention. No: it is an immeasurably deep well, an incomparably vast trek into uncharted territory abounding with unsurpassed intrigue. It is a welcome mat to higher reading; a beseeching of the mind to open its doors to innumerable wonders.

The characters are living. The threat is ominous. The purpose is clear. The terrain is vivid. The journey is meaningful. Middle-earth is a fortified treasury of rare gems and bounty, brimming over at every turn. The dialogues are rampant with skillful diction, and I cite especially the intense interchange of showdown between Gandalf and Saruman at the feet of Orthanc. The volley of interchange reflects Tolkien's deep prizing of intellectual and linguistic expression, and it is a lasting testament to his superb conversational mastery.

Overall, Middle-earth represents a place that deep in our hearts we would long to be a part of, to have some semblance of citizenship, if even for five minutes, or at the least, if even as a temporary observer for a flicker, a fraction of a second, to take in a lifetime of memories. Tolkien creates a world of sound logic and irrepressible imaginative girth. Middle-earth is highly plausible and *that*, in and of itself, sustains the story in intelligent mystique, and furthers our longing to be there.

If there ever was a Middle-earth, somewhere, sometime, it remains an artifact perfectly preserved in the well-known vault, the more-historical-than-fantastical record that is the epic literary and creative colossus, *The Lord of the Rings*.

Ode to Tolkien

An Original Poem
by Aaron Ryan

Ode to Tolkien

By Aaron Ryan

© 2025 Author Aaron Ryan

J.R.R. Tolkien had the most incredible rhyme and
meter in his poetic expressions.

The following poem, inspired by Tolkien's genius,
is my tribute to his legacy.

When heavy mist strayed in the dells
There came He weaving golden spells,
One Ring he wrought, and nineteen brought,
Up from the Sea, over the fells

In eyries safe above the Wold,
He boldly there His story told,
With palantír He far saw near
And gently wrought His world of old

A Silmaríl of ire and mirth

Descended He to Middle-earth

With flash and flames He gave them names

Empowering soul and spirit's birth

Elanor created He

And mallorn: towering, golden tree

Pale niphredil: He knew it well

From Númenor across the Sea

There flowering groves of iris grew

Forget-me-nots made soil blue

Within the vale there grew so frail

The evermind, nasturtiums too.

From Gulf of Lune to Nimrodel

Henneth Annûn to Rhosgobel

He gave them start by magic art

Mitheithel and Emyn Muil

Mithril He delved for under fount

In caverns deep beneath the mount

And golden jools: the bane of fools

For dragon's lust was paramount.

The first sapling of great Mirkwood

And foaming waters of Greyflood

These made He strong, and great their throng

And prospered them as He deemed good

Then made He Shire and Lorien

Hollin, Mount Mindolluin

And Morgul Vale wherein hearts fail

Past proud Gondor constructed then

Through down and fen of grassy Rohan

To set sail from Grey Havens then

From Amroth far to Gorgoroth

And Seven Streams of Lebennin

The tributaries of Anduin

Free from the ash of Orodruin

Past Argonath, Osgiliath

To Belfalas and back again

And Tol Brandir the isle of rock

Was leagues away from milky chalk

On stony hill of Bombadil

Still far from home of Brandybuck

With circlets silver, fillets gold

And flaxen-pale hair flowing cold:

Through these He birthed through Middle-

earth

Such beings as then would fit their mold

Mysterious made He Bombadil

Ere race was born of iron-will

Crying "Merry-O" and "Berry-O"

With River-Daughter drank their fill

He molded Elves and formed He men

In holes set halflings then therein

And Dwarves gave He to flowering sea

Of stone and quarry to chisel in

From acorn blessed He great Fangorn

From lineage crowned He Aragorn

In woods of gold from days of old:
Galadriel and Celeborn.

Sweet Rivendell He made for Elf
And for the Dwarf deep Dwarrowdelf
Then Isengard for Wizard hard
For Man the City of seven-shelf.

The Ents dwelt deep in Fangorn's core
As fire leapt up in Sammath Naur
Whilst dead of kin filled Rath Dínen
In Minas Tirith, in Gondor.

The Rohirrim, the Galadhrim
The Onodrim, the Sindarin
These made He flower in craft and power
To breathe out life from deep within

Great Gwaihir, eagle, Swift Windlord
And Asfaloth for flight to ford
The fell Cave-Troll, and drums that roll
In Moria where Balrog roared.

These made He well along with Grond

And Orcs led He across Morthond

But Southron dart went not to heart

Of Faramir nor Beregond.

'Tween Dwarves and Elves was kindled strife

Which segregated life from life

Deep Khazad-dûm and elvish moon

Were only close as blade of knife.

In spells unbroken dwelt the Wight

In barrows cold with pale light

Within their downs, they clinked their crowns

And lingered there by sleepless night.

Enclosed within Ephel Dúath

The Mountain vomits up its wrath

With blackened fume through hopeless gloom

He blanketed its cone with ash.

The Dark Lord Sauron of Mordor:

Him wreathed in smoke at Barad-dûr.

The Lidless Eye, vast shadow nigh,

The Nazgûl made He servants for

Three Rings for Elves under the sky
Nine unto men destined to die,
For Dwarves with stone, Seven were shone
And One for Sauron of the Lie.

The Ring was made to serve him well
Beyond all powers dark and fell
Perceived they all with grievous call:
Him they would fight with counterspell.

With great Elf-strength was crowned Elrond
And Elf-life stretched He overlong
The Last Alliance came in defiance
In vast array and armies strong

Isildur son of Elendil
Held sword that would be Andúril
Anárion, the other son
Fought not in vain, clean earth to till.

Unfurled they banners Elven-high

As standards broke beneath the sky

The hammer fell: Narsil's death-knell

And horror was the Dark Lord's cry.

Then Threw He down their Nemesis

Freed peoples unto genesis

The Ruling Ring: a vanished Thing

Until the ages should persist.

For Isildur came but never home

The Ring kept he unto his own

Him it betrayed, orcs him then slayed

The Ring passed into place unknown.

For it was Sauron's then no more

Thus Isildur avenged his fore

The foe was slain, his power wane

His spirit fled to darkened shore

The ages beat on timeless plain

The Ring: but a memory of pain

'Til then was found, deep underground

Sauron's heirloom yet once again

Along the banks of Anduin
There came two friends to frolic in
Déagol came and Sméagol same
But only one went home to kin.

For Déagol found the Ruling Ring
On River's bed, a pretty thing
But Sméagol craved, He Déagol graved
And Gollum came thus into being.

They called him names, he bit their feet
Then slunk he 'way to places deep
It him consumed in cold, dark tomb
'Til Bilbo came and stole from sleep

The Ring, and took it far away:
Dominion claimed him there that day.
'Til Wizard told of Shadow old
Whence came it unto Frodo's stay.

The Ringwraiths grasped their swords of steel

They smelt with nose that was not real

Yet living not, the Ring they sought:

With fervency of lust and will.

The Halfling stood, all folk came in

As Council forged a hope dread thin:

Would great Mount Doom become the tomb

For Sauron's Ring to vanish in?

There wisdom called for proper course

To purge the world of Sauron's force

In Mount Doom's fire, destroyed with ire

The Ring must return to its source.

The doom-bell rolled in Imladris

Whereas before was all amiss

The bane of all, with sunset's fall

On Frodo lay they burden this

A meddler in issues dire

'Twas Gandalf, slave of Secret Fire

He felt the Pit, and so was fit

To ravage foe with white-hot ire

Both Radagast and Mithrandir,

Subservient to Curunír

Survived the test as wizards, lest

They too become enslaved to fear.

Of Saruman He made craft fail

Before those last to leave set sail

His wisdom died, no more allied

With Elves nor Men through sad betrayal

Merry sent He and Peregrin

Then Boromir at Parth Galen

There paid his due, defending two

From Uruk-hai which captured them

The King of Rohan aged sat

Upon His throne in weakness that

Didst thin like air when Gandalf there

Spoke staves of healing and lifted threat

Then Rohan's lord with creak and crack

Thus straightened up his weathered back

He led the raid to Gondor's aid;
Tho' death and glory be his rack

On Shadowfax White Rider rode
The weary pilgrim less his load
And Glamdring rang as allies sang
When Mithrandir led Rohan's road

Yet Saruman was still to thwart
The Onodrim with doom came forth
The rock they ground with booming sound
And leveled Isengard by force

And all the while the brave twain went
With Eärendil's star the night was rent
Through Ithilien clear with Faramir
Frodo and Sam pursued their meant

But made He Gollum lust-filled trail
The faithful twain to Morgul Vale
Betrayed he them to Shelob's web
In Cirith Ungol Frodo paled.

For Gollum, Sméagol nevermore

Slave to "the precious," as he swore

He feigned reform, gave them to storm

In cold revenge he plotted gore

Then stout Samwise saved Frodo's keep

As he lay there by cliffs asleep

Sam bore his weight and kept his fate

Unto the fiery mountain deep.

But first would fealty take its toll

He rescued Frodo from Morgul

The sentinels passed, whereby at last

Came they to Mount Doom, weary in soul

Then one day war dyed red the skies

As light of battle filled the eyes

Of orcs and men in battle grim

With Minas Tirith as the prize.

The Witch-King fell with malice hard

O'er Théoden Éowyn stood her guard

Whilst Merry crept in Nazgûl's step

Before its head she clove ashard.

On fields of blood named Pelennor

There mighty names lived nevermore

They fought with pride, and so they died

To aid the Ringbearer in his chore

There Elf with bow and Dwarf with axe

And Gandalf upon Shadowfax

With Strider strode, Éomer rode

Them down, the orcs, to bloody wax.

With war abroad, the three alone:

Sam, Frodo pierced the Mountain's cone

At last the Ring, and suffering

Along with Gollum went unknown.

Then Barad-dûr the Mighty broke

The Dark Lord vanquished, up in smoke

He came to naught; his absence brought

To Middle-earth peace to all folk.

Thus from the broken line of Kings

Came Aragorn on silver wings

The Elfstone reigned, the Throne regained

By Dúnadan, once least of beings

And so was wrought the greatest tale

Of valiant life and death so pale

Thus Tolkien wove a tale that strove

To charge the mind and set the sails

On anvil smote He greatest note

Of yore which forged would cast the vote

The world amaze with bravest days

Of Middle-earth, of arms, His coat

And then He died but legend stayed

To tarry far beyond His day

Enchanting tale would never fail

To please the heart and lead the way…

Afterword

by Aaron Ryan

Afterword

The Lord of the Rings was the first literary work to move me. To reveal to me the possibilities of what a book could do.

To inspire me to become a writer in my own right, and to create, as Tolkien did.

As an author, I seek to write compelling works that take my reader away and provide a pleasant escapism from modern reality. I seek to whisk them of into a land with people and places that remain with them far after they've read the words *The End*. I strive to create settings and characters that my readers have a difficult time exorcising from their daily lives, and that blur the lines between reality and fiction.

I've strived to do this with my alien invasion hexalogy *Dissonance* as well as my Christian post-apocalyptic trilogy *The End*, both of which contain numerous tips of the hats and nods to Tolkien's prowess as the quintessential fantasy fiction writer.

Though I will never measure up and will always fall dreadfully short of his prowess, my lineage as a writer traces back to 1983, and, for the very first time, cracking open those musty, magic-laden pages that open with:

When Mr. Bilbo Baggins of Bag End announced that he would shortly be celebrating his eleventy-first birthday with a party of special magnificence, there was much talk and excitement in Hobbiton.

That first paragraph – and all of the ensuing ones – has held me captive and spellbound for forty long years of creativity and magic-making.

Please. ***Please*** do yourself a favor and read *The Lord of the Rings* before you outgrow belief. Don't grow too old to imagine. Middle-Earth *does* exist somewhere, sometime, and I encourage you to partake at once. The screen adaptations are wonderful to be sure, but there is nothing like the written word to compel you, draw you in, and stoke the embers of your own creativity as you imagine your way through this epic trilogy.

It is from a profound love of Tolkien's tremendous fantasy heavyweight that I have created not only all of my other works, but this book as well. Thank you for examining the best work of fantasy fiction there ever was, is, and evermore shall be.

Namarie,

Aaron Ryan

About the Author

Award-winning and bestselling author Aaron Ryan lives in Washington with his wife and two sons, along with Macy the dog, Winston the cat, and Merry & Pippin, the finches.

He is the author of the bestselling *Dissonance* 6-book alien invasion saga, the post-apocalyptic Christian fiction saga *The End*, the sci-fi thrillers *Forecast* and *The Slide*, *God is Not Santa,* the children's picture books *The Ring of Truth, The*

Sword of Joy and *The Book of Power*, the business reference books *How to Successfully Self-Publish & Promote Your Self-Published Book* and *The Superhero Anomaly*, 6 business books on voiceovers penned under his former stage name (Joshua Alexander), as well as a previous fictional novel, *The Omega Room.*

When he was in second grade, he was tasked with writing a creative assignment: a fictional book. And thus, *The Electric Boy* was born: a simple novella full of intrigue, fantasy, and 7-year-old wits that electrified Aaron's desire to write. From that point forward, Aaron evolved into a creative soul that desired to create.

He enjoys the arts, media, music, performing, poetry, and being a daddy. In his lifetime he has been an author, voiceover artist, wedding videographer, stage performer, musician, producer, rock/pop artist, executive assistant, service manager, paperboy, CSR, poet, tech support, worship leader, and more. The diversity of his life experiences gives him a unique approach to business, life, ministry, faith, and entertainment.

Aaron's favorite author by far is J.R.R. Tolkien, but he also enjoys Suzanne Collins, James S.A. Corey, Michael Crichton, Marie Lu, Madeleine L'Engle, John Grisham, Tom Clancy, C.S. Lewis, Stephen King and Dave Barry.

Aaron has always had a passion for storytelling. Visit his author website at www.authoraaronryan.com, the Dissonance post-apocalyptic alien invasion website at www.dissonancetheseries.com, or *The End* post-apocalyptic saga website at thisisnottheend.com.

If you liked this or any of Aaron's books, please visit the Amazon and Goodreads pages for the specific book(s) and leave a positive review. Once it shows up, please email the screenshot of it to me@authoraaronryan.com for a discount on your next book purchase from him! Thank you so much. Reviews really do help a ton!

Visit Aaron's website and sign up at the Blog:

Subscribe to Author Aaron Ryan

Follow Aaron and connect on Social Media:

Connect with Aaron

Feel free to check out the following links for further information on Aaron:

Subscribe to Aaron's blog for free giveaways, news and new releases at **authoraaronryan.com/blog**

Join the Author Aaron Ryan exclusive Facebook community at

facebook.com/groups/authoraaronryan

Subscribe to Aaron's YouTube channel at

youtube.com/@authoraaronryan

Visit Aaron's social media links to connect with him

at **dot.cards/authoraaronryan**

Also by the Author

As Aaron Ryan:

1. *The End: Alpha*

2. *The End: Omicron*

3. *The End: Omega*

4. *The End Christian Post-Apocalyptic Series*

5. *God Is Not Santa*

6. *The Ring of Truth*

7. *The Sword of Joy*

8. *The Book of Power*

9. *The Christian Kids Values, Identity & Affirmation Series*

10. *Dissonance Volume I: Reality*

11. *Dissonance Volume II: Reckoning*

12. *Dissonance Volume III: Renegade*

13. *Dissonance Volume IV: Relentless*

14. *Dissonance Volume Zero: Revelation*

15. *Dissonance Volume Up: Rising*

16. *The Complete Dissonance Sci-Fi Alien Invasion Saga*

17. *Forecast*

18. *The Slide*

19. *The Superhero Anomaly*

20. *How to Successfully Self-Publish & Promote Your Independent Book: A Self-Publishing & Business Marketing Guide For The Independent Author*

21. *Reflections: A Compilation of Journals and Poetry*

22. *The Omega Room (abandoned in the early 90's)*

23. *Autobiography (no longer available)*

24. *Glimmerings – works of poetry*

As his former stage name, Josh Alexander:

25. *Voiceovers: A Super Business, A Super Life*

26. *Voiceovers: A Super Fun Pursuit*

27. *Voiceovers: A Super Responsibility*